I Went To The Zoo

by
RITA GOLDEN GELMAN

illustrated by
MARYANN KOVALSKI

North Winds Press
A Division of Scholastic Canada Ltd.

For the paintings in this book, the illustrator used gouache and coloured pencil.

Book design by Kristina Iulo.
Cover design by Yüksel Hassan.

Canadian Cataloguing in Publication Data

Gelman, Rita Golden
    I went to the zoo

ISBN 0-590-74619-7

I. Kovalski, Maryann. II. Title.

PZ7.G46Iw 1993   j813'.54   C93-093045-2

6 5 4 3 2 1   Printed in USA   3 4 5 6 7/9

For Carolina, Francisco,
Carlos, and Isabel Restrepo,
Juan and Carolina Blanco Restrepo,
and their wonderful *abuela*,
Amparo Jaramillo.

R.G.G.

To Jenny, Joanna, and Gregory.

M.K.

The other day I went to the zoo.

I don't know why I went to the zoo.
It was a silly thing to do.
 The pandas were sitting.
 The camels were spitting.
They were as bored as bored could be.
"Come home," I said. "Come home
with me."

PLEASE
DON'T

The other day I went to the zoo.
I don't know why I went to the zoo.
It was a silly thing to do.
   The monkeys were swinging.
   Koalas were clinging.
   The pandas were sitting.
   The camels were spitting.
They were as bored as bored could be.
"Come home," I said. "Come home
with me."

PLEASE
DON'T FEED

The other day I went to the zoo.
I don't know why I went to the zoo.
It was a silly thing to do.
   The rabbits were hopping.
   The pigs were slopping.
   The monkeys were swinging.
   Koalas were clinging.
   The pandas were sitting.
   The camels were spitting.
They were as bored as bored could be.
"Come home," I said. "Come home
with me."

PLEASE
DON'T FEED

The other day I went to the zoo.
I don't know why I went to the zoo.
It was a silly thing to do.
    The penguins were sliding,
    The ostriches hiding.
    The rabbits were hopping.
    The pigs were slopping.
    The monkeys were swinging.
    Koalas were clinging.
    The pandas were sitting.
    The camels were spitting.
They were as bored as bored could be.
"Come home," I said. "Come home
with me."

PLEASE
DON'T FEED

The other day I went to the zoo.
I don't know why I went to the zoo.
It was a silly thing to do.

The horses were neighing,

The mantises praying.

The penguins were sliding,

The ostriches hiding.

The rabbits were hopping.

The pigs were slopping.

The monkeys were swinging.

Koalas were clinging.

The pandas were sitting.

The camels were spitting.

They were as bored as bored could be.
"Come home," I said. "Come home
with me."

PLEASE
DON'T FEED

The other day I went to the zoo.
I don't know why I went to the zoo.
It was a silly thing to do.
    The hippos were soaking.
    The bullfrogs were croaking.
    The horses were neighing,
    The mantises praying.
    The penguins were sliding,
    The ostriches hiding.
    The rabbits were hopping.
    The pigs were slopping.
    The monkeys were swinging.
    Koalas were clinging.
    The pandas were sitting.
    The camels were spitting.
They were as bored as bored could be.
"Come home," I said. "Come home
with me."

The other day I went to the zoo.
I don't know why I went to the zoo.
It was a silly thing to do.
 The beavers were slapping.
 The seals were clapping.
 The hippos were soaking.
 The bullfrogs were croaking.
 The horses were neighing,
 The mantises praying.
 The penguins were sliding,
 The ostriches hiding.
 The rabbits were hopping.
 The pigs were slopping.
 The monkeys were swinging.
 Koalas were clinging.
 The pandas were sitting.
 The camels were spitting.
They were as bored as bored could be.
"Come home," I said. "Come home
with me."

The other day I went to the zoo.
I don't know why I went to the zoo.
It was a silly thing to do.
  The tigers were crouching,
  The kangaroos pouching.
  The beavers were slapping.
  The seals were clapping.
  The hippos were soaking.
  The bullfrogs were croaking.
  The horses were neighing,
  The mantises praying.
  The penguins were sliding,
  The ostriches hiding.
  The rabbits were hopping.
  The pigs were slopping.
  The monkeys were swinging.
  Koalas were clinging.
  The pandas were sitting.
  The camels were spitting.
They were as bored as bored could be.
"Come home," I said. "Come home
with me."

The other day I went to the zoo.
I don't know why I went to the zoo.
It was a silly thing to do.
   The peacocks were posing,
   The elephants hosing.
   The tigers were crouching,
   The kangaroos pouching.
   The beavers were slapping.
   The seals were clapping.
   The hippos were soaking.
   The bullfrogs were croaking.
   The horses were neighing,
   The mantises praying.
   The penguins were sliding,
   The ostriches hiding.
   The rabbits were hopping.
   The pigs were slopping.
   The monkeys were swinging.
   Koalas were clinging.
   The pandas were sitting.
   The camels were spitting.
They were as bored as bored could be.
"Come home," I said. "Come home
with me."

The other day I went to the zoo.
I don't know why I went to the zoo.
It was a silly thing to do.

The wolves were howling.
The lions were growling.
The peacocks were posing,
The elephants hosing.
The tigers were crouching,
The kangaroos pouching.
The beavers were slapping.
The seals were clapping.
The hippos were soaking.
The bullfrogs were croaking.
The horses were neighing,
The mantises praying.
The penguins were sliding,
The ostriches hiding.
The rabbits were hopping.
The pigs were slopping.
The monkeys were swinging.
Koalas were clinging.
The pandas were sitting.
The camels were spitting.

They were as noisy and bored as could be.
"It's time," I said, "to come home
with me."

So two by two and three by three
I took the animals home with me.

As soon as the furniture started to break,
I knew I had made a big mistake.
They were sitting and spitting,
   swinging and clinging,
   hopping and slopping,
   sliding and hiding,
   neighing and praying,
   soaking and croaking,
   slapping and clapping,
   crouching and pouching,
   posing and hosing,
   howling and growling.
They were as messy as messy could be.
They couldn't, they shouldn't be home
with me!

So three by three,
And two by two,

I took the animals back to the zoo.

I don't know why I went to the zoo.
It was a *wonderful* thing to do.